lassy: A young girl.

yo-ho-ho: Hip-hip-hooray!

TE TALK

frilly dogs: Fancy-dressing dog pirates.

pieces of eight: Spanish dollars.

shiver me timbers: Well, that's a surprise!

BEST PIRATE

Written by
Kari-Lynn Winters

pajamapress

Illustrated by
Dean Griffiths

First published in Canada and the United States in 2017

Text copyright © 2017 Kari-Lynn Winters
Illustration copyright © 2017 Dean Griffiths
This edition copyright © 2017 Pajama Press Inc.
This is a first edition.

10 9 8 7 6 5 4 3 2 1

 Canada Council   Conseil des arts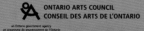
for the Arts   du Canada

The publisher gratefully acknowledges the support of the Canada Council for the Arts and
the Ontario Arts Council for its publishing program. We acknowledge the financial support
of the Government of Canada through the Canada Book Fund (CBF) for our publishing
activities.

Library and Archives Canada Cataloguing in Publication

Winters, Kari-Lynn, 1969-, author
     Best pirate / written by Kari-Lynn Winters ; illustrated
by Dean Griffiths.
ISBN 978-1-77278-019-2 (hardback)
     I. Griffiths, Dean, 1967-, illustrator II. Title.
PS8645.I5745B48 2017   jC813'.6   C2016-906084-5

Publisher Cataloging-in-Publication Data (U.S.)

Names: Winters, Kari-Lynn, 1969-, author. | Griffiths, Dean, 1967, illustrator.
Title: Best Pirate / written by Kari-Lynn Winters ; illustrated by Dean Griffiths.
Description: Toronto, Ontario, Canada: Pajama Press, 2017. |Summary:
"Scolded for being 'clumsy and kindly' instead of 'crafty and greedy', young
pirate Augusta becomes determined to prove herself by braving a scary
treasure hunt alone. When she and a member of a rival crew both get in
trouble, they disobey orders to work together and share the booty" —
Provided by publisher.
Identifiers: ISBN 978-1-77278-019-2 (hardcover)
Subjects: LCSH: Pirates – Juvenile fiction. | Dogs – Juvenile fiction. |Treasure
hunt (Game) – Juvenile fiction.| BISAC: JUVENILE FICTION / Action &
Adventure / Pirates. | JUVENILE FICTION / Social Themes / Values &
Virtues. | JUVENILE FICTION / Social Themes / Friendship.
Classification: LCC PZ7.W568Be |DDC [E] – dc23

Edited by Ann Featherstone
Designed by Rebecca Bender

Manufactured by Qualibre Inc./Print Plus
Printed in China

Pajama Press Inc.
181 Carlaw Ave. Suite 207 Toronto, Ontario Canada, M4M 2S1

Distributed in Canada by UTP Distribution
5201 Dufferin Street Toronto, Ontario Canada, M3H 5T8

Distributed in the U.S. by Ingram Publisher Services
1 Ingram Blvd. La Vergne, TN 37086, USA

We've gots to get the booty before them Tuna Lubbers!

We've gots to get the booty before them **Frilly Dogs!**

To me matey, Marco, for always making me a better pirate. And a shout-out to Claire, Aiden, Emily, and Kaz—a bunch of arr-some readers!

−K.L.W.

For my dad
−D.G.

Barnacle Garrick showed his daughter
a section of the treasure map.

Scully is crafty.
So he'll findz the booty
before them cats.

Augusta leaned
in closer.

He's nimble too. He'll sneak past
them Tuna Lubbers on Crossbones Island.

But most important, me lassy, Scully is **fearless.**
He'll pillage them doubloons and bring 'em back to our
ship—right where they needz to be.

Augusta moved the candle closer so her father could read the map better.

Barnacle growled a warning...but—

"Blimey! You ruined me map."

Now we'll never find the booty!
Augusta, you gots to be a **better** pirate!

She gots to be **nimble** and **fearless**—
not clumsy and afeard!

Scully eyed the remains
of the burnt map.

Barnacle stomped to
the hold.

Even though she didn't agree with her father's ways, Augusta practiced being

crafty,

nimble,

and **fearless**.

Everything was going well,
until...

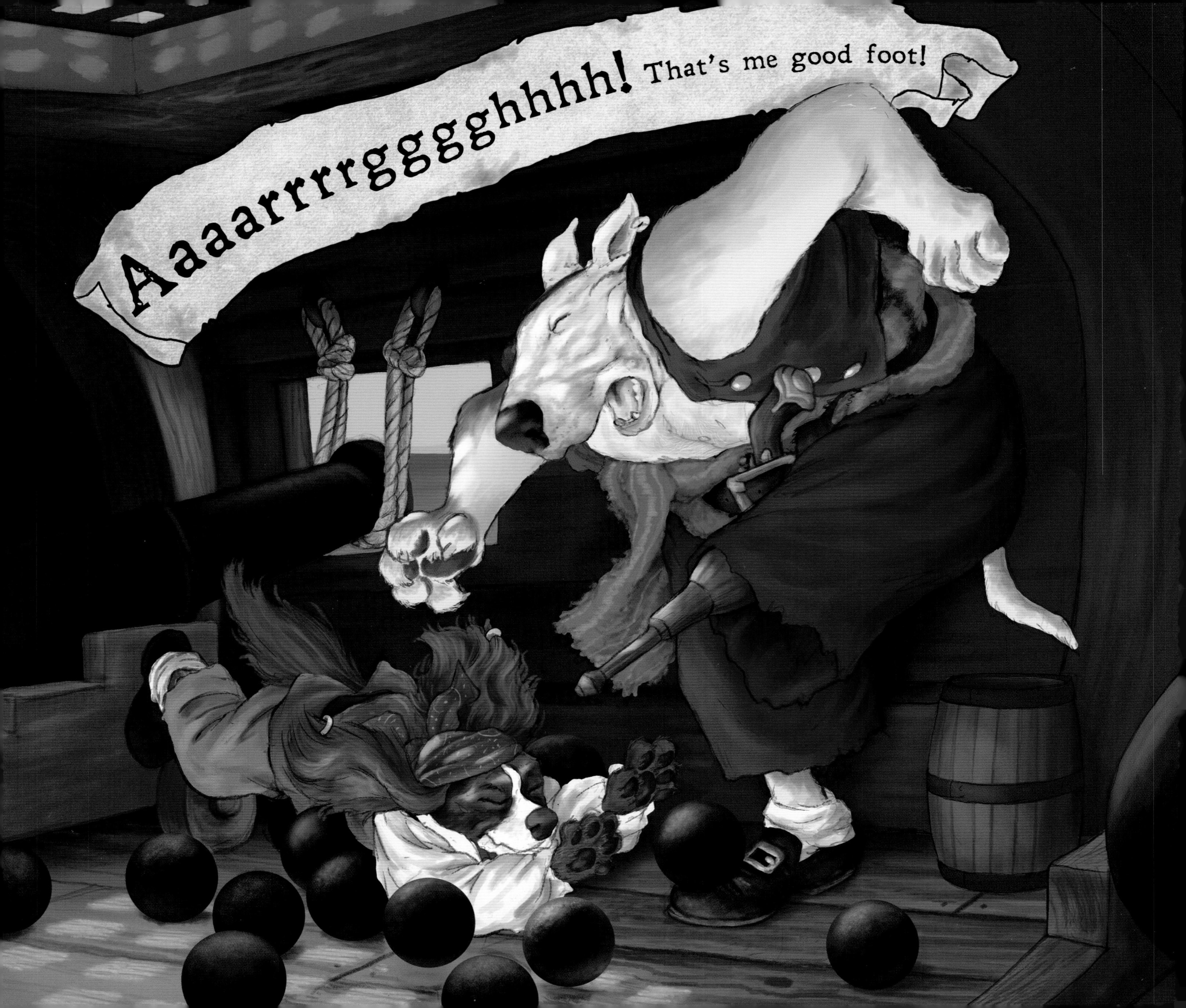
Aaaarrrrggggghhhh! That's me good foot!

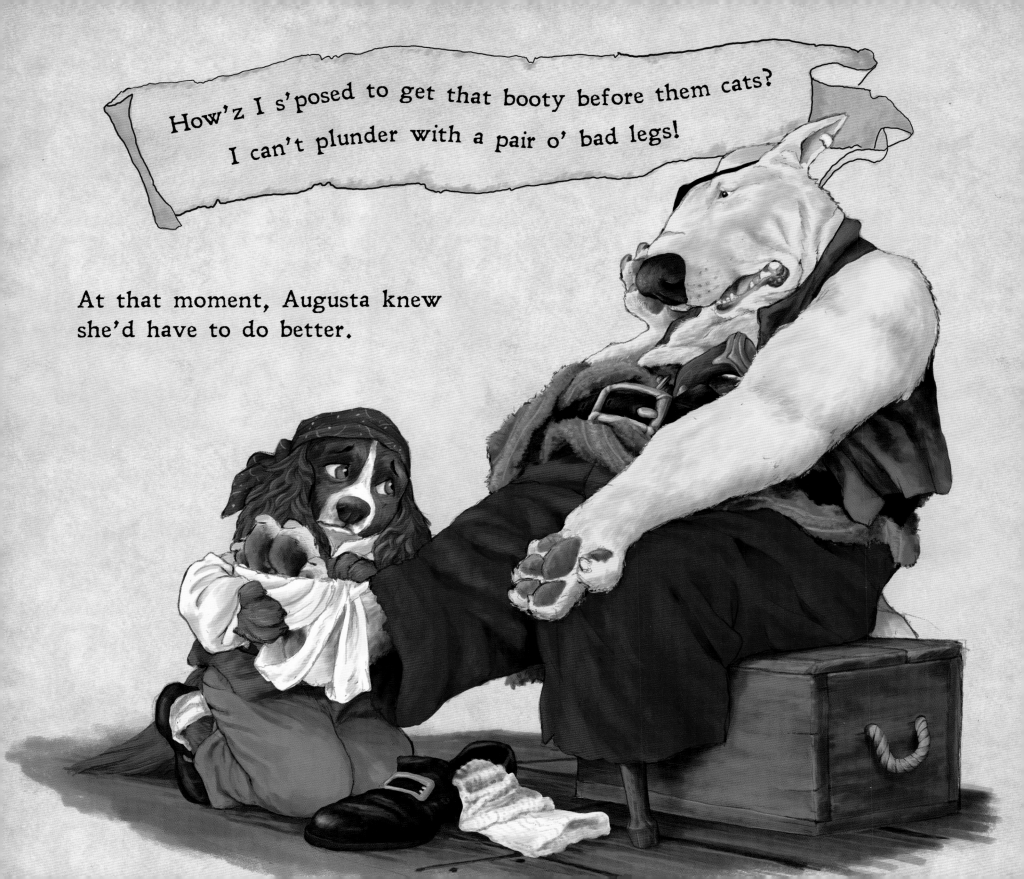

How'z I s'posed to get that booty before them cats?
I can't plunder with a pair o' bad legs!

At that moment, Augusta knew
she'd have to do better.

Early the next morning she prepared the jolly boat.

Squid and Bones tried to stop her.

Ye'll never find them doubloons with a burnt-up map!

The captain won't like this. It's too dangerous!

But Augusta announced:

I've hurt Scully. I have to make it right.

I'll bring the booty back myself.

The island was bigger and scarier than she expected.

Something moved.
Instead of acting afeard, Augusta stomped toward the sound.

You! You're one of those Tuna Lubbers!
You! Yez be one of them Frilly Dogs!

Suddenly—

Gimme that booty, you Tuna Lubber. It's mine!

Ye Frilly Dog. I'z be the **BEST** pirate! I should get the doubloons.

At that moment Augusta and Scuppers looked up—way up.

We gots to get out!

They tried reaching...

jumping...

and climbing...

Morning turned into afternoon.
Afternoon turned into evening.

Augusta was too, but she remembered she needed to be a better pirate—she needed to be **crafty**. So she devised a plan.

We'll never get out! I-I-I'z afeard.

She began collecting swords and daggers.

Avast, ye! Yez stole me sword! This is no time to pick a fight!

Augusta jammed the swords into the dirt walls.

Understanding her crafty plan, Scuppers offered his help.

Augusta and Scuppers worked quickly.
Soon, with their ditty bags full of booty,
they were climbing up and up. Augusta knew
she needed to be **nimble**.

Follow me!

As she climbed out of the hole, she felt **fearless**. But just then—

A dagger came loose.

Even though she was afeard, she reached out a paw and saved Scuppers.

Yez be the BEST pirate, Augusta.
The BEST pirate should get the doubloons.

We only made it out because we worked together.
Keep your half of the treasure.

And with their ditty bags and bandanas full,
the two mateys waved goodbye.

Augusta passed the doubloons to Scully.

Scully presented the treasure to Barnacle.

See, Augusta? Learn from the better pirate. Scully's crafty, nimble, and fearless. He seized our booty and outwitted them Tuna Lubbers.

Scully winked at Augusta.

Aye, Captain! We'z all be learnin' from the BEST.

NAUTICAL TALK

ditty bag: A small bag sailors use to carry their belongings.

hold: A space on the ship where the crew stores their cargo.

Captain: The boss of the ship.

maroon: Leave behind.

jolly boat: Rowboat.